THE RIOT AT COUGAR PAW

BY

ROBERT E. HOWARD

British Library Cataloguing-in-Publication Data
A catalogue record for this book is available from the
British Library

Robert E. Howard

Robert Ervin Howard was born in Peaster, Texas in 1906. During his youth, his family moved between a variety of Texan boomtowns, and Howard – a bookish and somewhat introverted child – was steeped in the violent myths and legends of the Old South. Although he loved reading and learning, Howard developed a distinctly Texan, hardboiled outlook on the world. He became a passionate fan of boxing, taking it up at an amateur level, and from the age of nine began to write adventure tales of semi-historical bloodshed. In 1919, when Howard was thirteen, his family moved to the Central Texas hamlet of Cross Plains, where he would stay for the rest of his life.

At fifteen Howard began to read the pulp magazines of the day, and to write more seriously. The December 1922 issue of his high school newspaper featured two of his stories, 'Golden Hope Christmas' and 'West is West'. In 1924 he sold his first piece – a short caveman tale titled 'Spear and Fang' – for $16 to the not-yet-famous *Weird Tales* magazine. He published with the magazine regularly over the next few years. 1929 was a breakout year for Howard, in that the 23-year-old writer began to sell to other magazines, such as *Ghost Stories* and *Argosy*, both of whom had previously sent him hundreds of rejection slips. In 1930, he began a correspondence with weird fiction master H. P. Lovecraft which ran up to his death six years later, and is regarded as one of the great correspondence cycles in all of fantasy literature.

It was partly due to Lovecraft's encouragement that Howard created his most famous character, Conan the Cimmerian. Conan – a barbarian-turned-King during the Hyborian Age, a mythical period of some 12,000 years ago – featured in seventeen *Weird Tales* stories between 1933 and 1936, and is now regarded as having spawned the 'sword and sorcery' genre, making Howard's influence on fantasy literature comparable to that of J. R. R. Tolkien's. The Conan stories have since been adapted many times, most famously in the series of films starring Arnold Schwarzenegger.

Howard was enjoying an all-time high in sales by the beginning of 1936, but he was also deeply upset by the ill health of his mother, who had fallen into a coma. On the morning of June 11, 1936, he asked an attending nurse whether she would ever recover, and the nurse replied negatively. Howard walked to his car, parked outside the family home in Cross Plains, and shot himself. He died eight hours later, aged just thirty.

I was out in the blacksmith shop by the corral beating out some shoes for Cap'n Kidd, when my brother John come sa'ntering in. He'd been away for a few weeks up in the Cougar Paw country, and he'd evidently done well, whatever he'd been doing, because he was in a first class humor with hisself, and plumb spilling over with high spirits and conceit. When he feels prime like that he wants to rawhide everybody he meets, especially me. John thinks he's a wit, but I figger he's just half right.

"Air you slavin' over a hot forge for that mangy, flea-bit hunk of buzzard-meat again?" he greeted me. "That broom-tail ain't wuth the iron you wastes on his splayed-out hooves!"

He knows the easiest way to git under my hide is to poke fun at Cap'n Kidd. But I reflected it was just envy on his part, and resisted my natural impulse to bend the tongs over his head. I taken the white-hot iron out of the forge and put it on the anvil and started beating it into shape with the sixteen-pound sledge I always uses. I got no use for the toys which most blacksmiths uses for hammers.

"If you ain't got nothin' better to do than criticize a animal which is a damn sight better hoss than you'll ever be a man," I said with dignerty, between licks, "I calls yore attention to a door right behind you which nobody ain't usin' at the moment."

3

He bust into loud rude laughter and said: "You call that thing a hossshoe? It's big enough for a snow plow! Here, long as yo're in the business, see can you fit a shoe for that!"

He sot his foot up on the anvil and I give it a good slam with the hammer. John let out a awful holler and begun hopping around over the shop and cussing fit to curl yore hair. I kept on hammering my iron.

Just then pap stuck his head in the door and beamed on us, and said: "You boys won't never grow up! Always playin' yore childish games, and sportin' in yore innercent frolics!"

"He's busted my toe," said John blood-thirstily, "and I'll have his heart's blood if it's the last thing I do."

"Chips off the old block," beamed pap. "It takes me back to the time when, in the days of my happy childhood, I emptied a sawed-off shotgun into the seat of brother Joel's britches for tellin' our old man it was me which put that b'ar-trap in his bunk."

"He'll rue the day," promised John, and hobbled off to the cabin with moans and profanity. A little later, from his yells, I gathered that he had persuaded maw or one of the gals to rub his toe with hoss-liniment. He could make more racket about nothing then any Elkins I ever knowed.

I went on and made the shoes and put 'em on Cap'n Kidd, which is a job about like roping and hawg-tying a mountain cyclone, and by the time I got through and went up to the cabin to eat, John seemed to have got over his mad spell. He was laying on his bunk with his foot up on it all bandaged up, and he says: "Breckinridge, they ain't no use in grown men holdin' a grudge. Let's fergit about it."

"Who's holdin' any grudge?" I ast, making sure he didn't have a bowie knife in his left hand. "I dunno why they should be so much racket over a trifle that didn't amount to nothin', nohow."

"Well," he said, "this here busted foot discommodes me a heap. I won't be able to ride for a day or so, and they is business up to Cougar Paw I ought to 'tend to."

"I thought you just come from there," I says.

"I did," he said, "but they is a man up there which has promised me somethin' which is due me, and now I ain't able to go collect. Whyn't you go collect for me, Breckinridge? You ought to, dern it, because its yore fault I cain't ride. The man's name is Bill Santry, and he lives up in the mountains a few miles from Cougar Paw. You'll likely find him in Cougar Paw any day, though."

"What's this he promised you?" I ast.

"Just ask for Bill Santry," he said. "When you find him say to him: 'I'm John Elkins' brother, and you can give me what you promised him.'"

My family always imposes onto my good nature; generally I'd rather go do what they want me to do than to go to the trouble with arguing with 'em.

"Oh, all right," I said. "I ain't got nothin' to do right now."

"Thanks, Breckinridge," he said. "I knowed I could count on you."

SO A COUPLE OF DAYS later I was riding through the Cougar Range, which is very thick-timbered mountains, and rapidly approaching Cougar Paw. I hadn't never been there before, but I was follering a winding wagon-road which I knowed would eventually fetch me there.

The road wound around the shoulder of a mountain, and ahead of me I seen a narrer path opened into it, and just before I got there I heard a bull beller, and a gal screamed: "Help! Help! Old Man Kirby's bull's loose!"

They came a patter of feet, and behind 'em a smashing and crashing in the underbrush, and a gal run out of the path into the road, and a rampaging bull was right behind her with his head lowered to toss her. I reined Cap'n Kidd between her and him, and knowed Cap'n Kidd would do the rest without no advice from me. He done so by wheeling and lamming his heels into that bull's ribs so hard he kicked the critter clean through a rail fence on the other side of the road. Cap'n Kidd hates bulls, and he's too big and strong for any of 'em. He would of then jumped on the critter and stomped him, but I restrained him, which made him mad, and whilst he was trying to buck me off, the bull ontangled

6

hisself and high-tailed it down the mountain, bawling like a scairt yearling.

When I had got Cap'n Kidd in hand, I looked around and seen the gal looking at me very admiringly. I swept off my Stetson and bowed from my saddle and says: "Can I assist you any father, m'am?"

She blushed purty as a pitcher and said: "I'm much obliged, stranger. That there critter nigh had his hooks into my hide. Whar you headin'? If you ain't in no hurry I'd admire to have you drop by the cabin and have a snack of b'ar meat and honey. We live up the path about a mile."

They ain't nothin' I'd ruther do," I assured her. "But just at the present I got business in Cougar Paw. How far is it from here?"

"'Bout five mile down the road," says she. "My name's Joan; what's yore'n?"

"Breckinridge Elkins, of Bear Creek," I said. "Say, I got to push on to Cougar Paw, but I'll be ridin' back this way tomorrer mornin' about sun-up. If you could--"

"I'll be waitin' right here for you," she said so promptly it made my head swim. No doubt about it; it was love at first sight. "I--I got store-bought shoes," she added shyly. "I'll be a-wearin' 'em when you come along."

"I'll be here if I have to wade through fire, flood and hostile Injuns," I assured her, and rode on down the wagon-trace with my manly heart swelling with pride in my bosom.

They ain't many mountain men which can awake the fire of love in a gal's heart at first sight--a gal, likewise, which was as beautiful as that there gal, and rich enough to own store-bought shoes. As I told Cap'n Kidd, they was just something about a Elkins.

It was about noon when I rode into Cougar Paw which was a tolerably small village sot up amongst the mountains, with a few cabins where folks lived, and a few more which was a grocery store and a jail and a saloon. Right behind the saloon was a good-sized cabin with a big sign onto it which said: Jonathan Middleton, Mayor of Cougar Paw.

They didn't seem to be nobody in sight, not even on the saloon porch, so I rode on to the corrals which served for a livery stable and wagon yard, and a man come out of the cabin nigh it, and took charge of Cap'n Kidd. He wanted to turn him in with a couple of mules which hadn't never been broke, but I knowed what Cap'n Kidd would do to them mules, so the feller give him a corral to hisself, and belly-ached just because Cap'n Kidd playfully bit the seat out of his britches.

He ca'med down when I paid for the britches. I ast him where I could find Bill Santry, and he said likely he was up to the store.

SO I WENT UP TO THE store, and it was about like all them stores you see in them kind of towns--groceries, and dry-goods, and grindstones, and harness and such-like stuff,

and a wagon-tongue somebody had mended recent. They
warn't but the one store in the town and it handled a little
of everything. They was a sign onto it which said: General
Store; Jonathan Middleton, Prop.

They was a bunch of fellers setting around on goods
boxes and benches eating sody crackers and pickles out of
a barrel, and they was a tolerable hard-looking gang. I said:
"I'm lookin' for Bill Santry."

The biggest man in the store, which was setting on
a bench, says: "You don't have to look no farther. I'm Bill
Santry."

"Well," I says, "I'm Breckinridge Elkins, John Elkins'
brother. You can give me what you promised him."

"Ha!" he says with a snort like a hungry catamount
rising sudden. "They is nothin' which could give me more
pleasure! Take it with my blessin'!" And so saying he picked
up the wagon tongue and splintered it over my head.

It was so onexpected that I lost my footing and fell on
my back, and Santry give a wolfish yell and jumped into my
stummick with both feet, and the next thing I knowed nine
or ten more fellers was jumping up and down on me with
their boots.

Now I can take a joke as well as the next man, but it
always did make me mad for a feller to twist a spur into my
hair and try to tear the sculp off. Santry having did this, I
throwed off them lunatics which was trying to tromp out my

innards, and riz up amongst them with a outraged beller. I swept four or five of 'em into my arms and give 'em a grizzly-hug, and when I let go all they was able to do was fall on the floor and squawk about their busted ribs.

I then turned onto the others which was assaulting me with pistols and bowie knives and the butt ends of quirts and other villainous weppins, and when I laid into 'em you should of heard 'em howl. Santry was trying to dismember my ribs with a butcher knife he'd got out of the pork barrel, so I picked up the pickle barrel and busted it over his head. He went to the floor under a avalanche of splintered staves and pickles and brine, and then I got hold of a grindstone and really started getting destructive. A grindstone is a good comforting implement to have hold of in a melee, but kind of clumsy. For instance when I hove it at a feller which was trying to cock a sawed-off shotgun, it missed him entirely and knocked all the slats out of the counter and nigh squashed four or five men which was trying to shoot me from behind it. I settled the shotgun-feller's hash with a box of canned beef, and then I got hold of a double-bitted axe, and the embattled citizens of Cougar Paw quit the field with blood-curdling howls of fear--them which was able to quit and howl.

I stumbled over the thickly-strewn casualties to the door, taking a few casual swipes at the shelves as I went past, and knocking all the cans off of them. Just as I emerged into the street, with my axe lifted to chop down anybody which opposed me, a skinny looking human bobbed up in front of me and hollered: "Halt, in the name of the law!"

Paying no attention to the double-barreled shotgun he shoved in my face, I swung back my axe for a swipe, and accidentally hit the sign over the door and knocked it down on top of him. He let out a squall as he went down and let bam! with the shotgun right in my face so close it singed my eyebrows. I pulled the sign-board off of him so I could git a good belt at him with my axe, but he hollered: "I'm the sheriff! I demands that you surrenders to properly constupated authority!"

I then noticed that he had a star pinned onto one gallus, so I put down my axe and let him take my guns. I never resists a officer of the law--well, seldom ever, that is.

He p'inted his shotgun at me and says: "I fines you ten dollars for disturbin' the peace!"

About this time a lanky maverick with side-whiskers come prancing around the corner of the building, and he started throwing fits like a locoed steer.

"The scoundrel's rooint my store!" he howled. "He's got to pay me for the counters and winders he busted, and the shelves he knocked down, and the sign he rooint, and the pork-keg he busted over my clerk's head!"

"What you think he ought to pay, Mr. Middleton?" ast the sheriff.

11

"Five hundred dollars," said the mayor bloodthirstily.

"Five hundred hell!" I roared, stung to wrath. "This here whole dern town ain't wuth five hundred dollars. Anyway, I ain't got no money but fifty cents I owe to the feller that runs the wagon yard."

"Gimme the fifty cents," ordered the mayor. "I'll credit that onto yore bill."

"I'll credit my fist onto yore skull," I snarled, beginning to lose my temper, because the butcher knife Bill Santry had carved my ribs with had salt on the blade, and the salt got into the cuts and smarted. "I owes this fifty cents and I gives it to the man I owes it to."

"Throw him in jail!" raved Middleton. "We'll keep him there till we figures out a job of work for him to do to pay out his fine."

So the sheriff marched me down the street to the log cabin which they used for a jail, whilst Middleton went moaning around the rooins of his grocery store, paying no heed to the fellers which lay groaning on the floor. But I seen the rest of the citizens packing them out on stretchers to take 'em into the saloon to bring 'em to. The saloon had a sign; Square Deal Saloon; Jonathan Middleton, Prop. And I heard fellers cussing Middleton because he made 'em pay for the licker they poured on the victims' cut and bruises. But they cussed under their breath. Middleton seemed to pack a lot of power in that there town.

Well, I laid down on the jail-house bunk as well as I could, because they always build them bunks for ordinary-sized men about six foot tall, and I wondered what in hell Bill Santry had hit me with that wagon tongue for. It didn't seem to make no sense.

I laid there and waited for the sheriff to bring me my supper, but he didn't bring none, and purty soon I went to sleep and dreamed about Joan, with her store-bought shoes.

What woke me up was a awful racket in the direction of the saloon. I got up and looked out of the barred winder. Night had fell, but the cabins and the saloon was well lit up, but too far away for me to tell what was going on. But the noise was so familiar I thought for a minute I must be back on Bear Creek again, because men was yelling and cussing, and guns was banging, and a big voice roaring over the din. Once it sounded like somebody had got knocked through a door, and it made me right home-sick, it was so much like a dance on Bear Creek.

I pulled the bars out of the winder trying to see what was going on, but all I could see was what looked like men flying headfirst out of the saloon, and when they hit the ground and stopped rolling, they jumped up and run off in all directions, hollering like the Apaches was on their heels.

Purty soon I seen somebody running toward the jail as hard as he could leg it, and it was the sheriff. Most of his

13

clothes was tore off, and he had blood on his face, and he was gasping and panting.

"We got a job for you, Elkins!" he panted. "A wild man from Texas just hit town, and is terrorizin' the citizens! If you'll pertect us, and layout this fiend from the prairies, we'll remit yore fine! Listen at that!"

From the noise I jedged the aforesaid wild man had splintered the panels out of the bar.

"What started him on his rampage?" I ast.

"Aw, somebody said they made better chili con carne in Santa Fe than they did in El Paso," says the sheriff. "So this maneyack starts cleanin' up the town--"

"Well, I don't blame him," I said. "That was a dirty lie and a low-down slander. My folks all come from Texas, and if you Cougar Paw coyotes thinks you can slander the State and git away with it--"

"We don't think nothin'!" wailed the sheriff, wringing his hands and jumping like a startled deer every time a crash resounded up the street. "We admits the Lone Star State is the cream of the West in all ways! Lissen, will you lick this homicidal lunatic for us? You got to, dern it. You got to work out yore fine, and--"

"Aw, all right," I said, kicking the door down before he could unlock it. "I'll do it. I cain't waste much time in this town. I got a engagement down the road tomorrer at sun-up."

The street was deserted, but heads was sticking out of every door and winder. The sheriff stayed on my heels till I was a few feet from the saloon, and then he whispered: "Go to it, and make it a good job! If anybody can lick that grizzly in there, it's you!" He then ducked out of sight behind the nearest cabin after handing me my gun-belt.

I stalked into the saloon and seen a gigantic figger standing at the bar and just fixing to pour hisself a dram out of a demijohn. He had the place to hisself, but it warn't near as much of a wreck as I'd expected.

As I come in he wheeled with a snarl, as quick as a cat, and flashing out a gun. I drawed one of mine just as quick, and for a second we stood there, glaring at each other over the barrels.

"Breckinridge Elkins!" says he. "My own flesh and blood kin!"

"Cousin Bearfield Buckner!" I says, shoving my gun back in its scabbard. "I didn't even know you was in Nevada."

"I GOT A RAMBLIN' FOOT," says he, holstering his shooting iron. "Put 'er there, Cousin Breckinridge!"

"By golly, I'm glad to see you!" I said, shaking with him. Then I recollected. "Hey!" I says. "I got to lick you."

"What you mean?" he demanded.

"Aw," I says, "I got arrested, and ain't got no money to pay my fine, and I got to work it out. And lickin' you was the job they gimme."

"I ain't got no use for law," he said grumpily. "Still and all, if I had any dough, I'd pay yore fine for you."

"A Elkins don't accept no charity," I said slightly nettled. "We works for what we gits. I pays my fine by lickin' the hell out of you, Cousin Bearfield."

At this he lost his temper; he was always hot-headed that way. His black brows come down and his lips curled up away from his teeth and he clenched his fists which was about the size of mallets.

"What kind of kinfolks air you?" he scowled. "I don't mind a friendly fight between relatives, but yore intentions is mercenary and unworthy of a true Elkins. You put me in mind of the fact that yore old man had to leave Texas account of a hoss gittin' its head tangled in a lariat he was totin' in his absent-minded way."

"That there is a cussed lie," I said with heat. "Pap left Texas because he wouldn't take the Yankee oath after the Civil War, and you know it. Anyway," I added bitingly, "nobody can ever say a Elkins ever stole a chicken and roasted it in a chaparral thicket."

He started violently and turned pale.

"What you hintin' at, you son of Baliol?" he hollered.

"Yore iniquities ain't no family secret," I assured him bitterly. "Aunt Atascosa writ Uncle Jeppard Grimes about you stealin' that there Wyandotte hen off of Old Man Westfall's roost."

16

"Shet up!" he bellered, jumping up and down in his wrath, and clutching his six-shooters convulsively. "I war just a yearlin' when I lifted that there fowl and et it, and I war plumb famished, because a posse had been chasin' me six days. They was after me account of Joe Richardson happenin' to be in my way when I was emptyin' my buffalo rifle. Blast yore soul, I have shot better men than you for talkin' about chickens around me."

"Nevertheless," I said, "the fact remains that yo're the only one of the clan which ever swiped a chicken. No Elkins never stole no hen."

"No," he sneered, "they prefers hosses."

Just then I noticed that a crowd had gathered timidly outside the doors and winders and was listening eagerly to this exchange of family scandals, so I said: "We've talked enough. The time for action has arriv. When I first seen you, Cousin Bearfield, the thought of committin' mayhem onto you was very distasteful. But after our recent conversation, I feels I can scramble yore homely features with a free and joyful spirit. Le's have a snort and then git down to business."

"Suits me," he agreed, hanging his gun belt on the bar. "Here's a jug with about a gallon of red licker into it."

So we each taken a medium-sized snort, which of course emptied the jug, and then I hitched my belt and says: "Which does you desire first, Cousin Bearfield--a busted laig or a fractured skull?"

"Wait a minute," he requested as I approached him. "What's, that on yore boot?"

I stooped over to see what it was, and he swung his laig and kicked me in the mouth as hard as he could, and imejitately busted into a guffaw of brutal mirth. Whilst he was thus employed I spit his boot out and butted him in the belly with a vi'lence which changed his haw-haw to a agonized grunt, and then we laid hands on each other and rolled back and forth acrost the floor, biting and gouging, and that was how the tables and chairs got busted. Mayor Middleton must of been watching through a winder because I heard him squall: "My Gawd, they're wreckin' my saloon! Sheriff, arrest 'em both."

And the sheriff hollered back: "I've took yore orders all I aim to, Jonathan Middleton! If you want to stop that double-cyclone git in there and do it yoreself!"

Presently we got tired scrambling around on the floor amongst the cuspidors, so we riz simultaneous and I splintered the roulette wheel with his carcass, and he hit me on the jaw so hard he knocked me clean through the bar and all the bottles fell off the shelves and showered around me, and the ceiling lamp come loose and spilled about a gallon of red hot ile down his neck.

Whilst he was employed with the ile I clumb up from among the debris of the bar and started my right fist in a swing from the floor, and after it traveled maybe nine feet it took Cousin Bearfield under the jaw, and he hit the oppersite wall so hard he knocked out a section and went clean through it, and that was when the roof fell in.

I started kicking and throwing the rooins off me, and then I was aware of Cousin Bearfield lifting logs and beams off of me, and in a minute I crawled out from under 'em.

"I could of got out all right," I said. "But just the same I'm much obleeged to you."

"Blood's thicker'n water," he grunted, and hit me under the jaw and knocked me about seventeen feet backwards toward the mayor's cabin. He then rushed forward and started kicking me in the head, but I riz up in spite of his efforts.

"Git away from that cabin!" screamed the mayor, but it was too late. I hit Cousin Bearfield between the eyes and he crashed into the mayor's rock chimney and knocked the whole base loose with his head, and the chimney collapsed and the rocks come tumbling down on him.

BUT BEING A TEXAS BUCKNER, Bearfield riz out of the rooins. He not only riz, but he had a rock in his hand about the size of a watermelon and he busted it over my head. This infuriated me, because I seen he had no intention of fighting fair, so I tore a log out of the wall of the mayor's cabin and belted him over the ear with it, and Cousin Bearfield bit the dust. He didn't git up that time.

19

Whilst I was trying to git my breath back and shaking the sweat out of my eyes, all the citizens of Cougar Paw come out of their hiding places and the sheriff yelled: "You done a good job, Elkins! Yo're a free man!"

"He is like hell!" screamed Mayor Middleton, doing a kind of war-dance, whilst weeping and cussing together. "Look at my cabin! I'm a rooint man! Sheriff, arrest that man!"

"Which 'un?" inquired the sheriff.

"The feller from Texas," said Middleton bitterly. "He's unconscious, and it won't be no trouble to drag him to jail. Run the other'n out of town. I don't never want to see him no more."

"Hey!" I said indignantly. "You cain't arrest Cousin Bearfield. I ain't goin' to stand for it."

"Will you resist a officer of the law?" ast the sheriff, sticking his gallus out on his thumb.

"You represents the law whilst you wear yore badge?" I inquired.

"As long as I got that badge on," boasts he, "I am the law!"

"Well," I said, spitting on my hands, "you ain't got it on now. You done lost it somewhere in the shuffle tonight, and you ain't nothin' but a common citizen like me! Git ready, for I'm comin' head-on and wide-open!"

I whooped me a whoop.

He glanced down in a stunned sort of way at his empty gallus, and then he give a scream and took out up the street with most of the crowd streaming out behind him.

"Stop, you cowards!" screamed Mayor Middleton. "Come back here and arrest these scoundrels--"

"Aw, shet up," I said disgustedly, and give him a kind of push and how was I to know it would dislocate his shoulder blade. It was just beginning to git light by now, but Cousin Bearfield wasn't showing no signs of consciousness, and I heard them Cougar Paw skunks yelling to each other back and forth from the cabins where they'd forted themselves, and from what they said I knowed they figgered on opening up on us with their Winchesters as soon as it got light enough to shoot good.

Just then I noticed a wagon standing down by the wagon-yard, so I picked up Cousin Bearfield and lugged him down there and throwed him into the wagon. Far be it from a Elkins to leave a senseless relative to the mercy of a Cougar Paw mob. I went into the corral where them two wild mules was and started putting harness onto 'em, and it warn't no child's play. They hadn't never been worked before, and they fell onto me with a free and hearty enthusiasm. Onst they had me down stomping on me, and the citizens of Cougar Paw made a kind of half-hearted sally. But I unlimbered my .45s and throwed a few slugs in their direction and they all hollered and run back into their cabins.

I finally had to stun them fool mules with a bat over the ear with my fist, and before they got their senses back, I had 'em harnessed to the wagon, and Cap'n Kidd and Cousin Bearfield's hoss tied to the rear end.

"He's stealin' our mules!" howled somebody, and taken a wild shot at me, as I headed down the street, standing up in the wagon and keeping them crazy critters straight by sheer strength on the lines.

"I ain't stealin' nothin'!" I roared as we thundered past the cabins where spurts of flame was already streaking out of the winders. "I'll send this here wagon and these mules back tomorrer!"

The citizens answered with blood-thirsty yells and a volley of lead, and with their benediction singing past my ears, I left Cougar Paw in a cloud of dust and profanity.

THEM MULES, AFTER A vain effort to stop and kick loose from the harness, laid their bellies to the ground and went stampeding down that crooking mountain road like scairt jackrabbits. We went around each curve on one wheel, and sometimes we'd hit a stump that would throw the whole wagon several foot into the air, and that must of been what brung Cousin Bearfield to hisself. He was laying sprawled in the bed, and finally we taken a bump that throwed him in a somersault clean to the other end of the wagon. He hit on his neck and riz up on his hands and knees and looked around dazedly at the trees and stumps which was flashing

past, and bellered: "What the hell's happenin'? Where-at am
I, anyway?"

"Yo're on yore way to Bear Creek, Cousin Bearfield!"
I yelled, cracking my whip over them fool mules' backs.
"Yippee ki-yi! This here is fun, ain't it, Cousin Bearfield?"

I was thinking of Joan waiting with her store-bought
shoes for me down the road, and in spite of my cuts and
bruises, I was rolling high and handsome.

"Slow up!" roared Cousin Bearfield, trying to stand up.
But just then we went crashing down a steep bank, and the
wagon tilted, throwing Cousin Bearfield to the other end
of the wagon where he rammed his head with great force
against the front-gate. "#$%&*?@!" says Cousin Bearfield.
"Glug!" Because we had hit the creek bed going full speed
and knocked all the water out of the channel, and about a
hundred gallons splashed over into the wagon and nearly
washed Cousin Bearfield out.

"If I ever git out of this alive," promised Cousin
Bearfield, "I'll kill you if it's the last thing I do--"

But at that moment the mules stampeded up the bank
on the other side and Cousin Bearfield was catapulted to
the rear end of the wagon so hard he knocked out the end-
gate with his head and nearly went out after it, only he just
managed to grab hisself.

We went plunging along the road and the wagon
hopped from stump to stump and sometimes it crashed

through a thicket of bresh. Cap'n Kidd and the other hoss was thundering after us, and the mules was braying and I was whooping and Cousin Bearfield was cussing, and purty soon I looked back at him and hollered: "Hold on, Cousin Bearfield! I'm goin' to stop these critters. We're close to the place where my gal will be waitin' for me--"

"Look out, you blame fool!" screamed Cousin Bearfield, and then the mules left the road and went one on each side of a white oak tree, and the tongue splintered, and they run right out of the harness and kept high-tailing it, but the wagon piled up on that tree with a jolt that throwed me and Cousin Bearfield headfirst into a blackjack thicket.

Cousin Bearfield vowed and swore, when he got back home, that I picked this thicket special on account of the hornets' nest that was there, and drove into it plumb deliberate. Which same is a lie which I'll stuff down his gizzard next time I cut his sign. He claimed they was trained hornets which I educated not to sting me, but the fact was I had sense enough to lay there plumb quiet. Cousin Bearfield was fool enough to run.

Well, he knows by this time, I reckon, that the fastest man afoot can't noways match speed with a hornet. He taken out through the bresh and thickets, yelpin' and hollerin' and hoppin' most bodacious. He run in a circle, too, for in three minutes he come bellerin' back, gave one last hop and dove back into the thicket. By this time I figgered he'd wore the hornets out, so I came alive again.

I extricated myself first and locating Cousin Bearfield by his profanity, I laid hold onto his hind laig and pulled him out. He lost most of his clothes in the process, and his temper wasn't no better. He seemed to blame me for his misfortunes.

"Don't tech me," he said fiercely. "Leave me be. I'm as close to Bear Creek right now as I want to be. Whar's my hoss?"

The hosses had broke loose when the wagon piled up, but they hadn't gone far, because they was fighting with each other in the middle of the road. Bearfield's hoss was about as big and mean as Cap'n Kidd. We separated 'em and Bearfield clumb aboard without a word.

"Where you goin', Cousin Bearfield?" I ast.

"As far away from you as I can," he said bitterly. "I've saw all the Elkinses I can stand for awhile. Doubtless yore intentions is good, but a man better git chawed by lions than rescued by a Elkins!"

And with a few more observations which highly shocked me, and which I won't repeat, he rode off at full speed, looking very pecooliar, because his pants was about all that hadn't been tore off of him, and he had scratches and bruises all over him.

I WAS SORRY COUSIN Bearfield was so sensitive, but I didn't waste no time brooding over his ingratitude. The sun was up and I knowed Joan would be waiting for me where the path come down into the road from the mountain.

Sure enough, when I come to the mouth of the trail, there she was, but she didn't have on her store-bought shoes, and she looked flustered and scairt.

"Breckinridge!" she hollered, running up to me before I could say a word. "Somethin' terrible's happened! My brother was in Cougar Paw last night, and a big bully beat him up somethin' awful! Some men are bringin' him home on a stretcher! One of 'em rode ahead to tell me!"

"How come I didn't pass 'em on the road?" I said, and she said: "They walked and taken a short cut through the hills. There they come now."

I seen some men come into the road a few hundred yards away and come toward us, lugging somebody on a stretcher like she said.

"Come on!" she says, tugging at my sleeve. "Git down off yore hoss and come with me. I want him to tell you who done it, so you can whup the scoundrel!"

"I got a idee, I know who done it," I said, climbing down. "But I'll make sure." I figgered it was one of Cousin Bearfield's victims.

"Why, look!" said Joan. "How funny the men are actin' since you started toward 'em! They've sot down the litter and

26

they're runnin' off into the woods! Bill!" she shrilled as we drawed nigh. "Bill, air you hurt bad?"

"A busted laig and some broke ribs," moaned the victim on the litter, which also had his head so bandaged I didn't recognize him. Then he sot up with a howl. "What's that ruffian doin' with you?" he roared, and to my amazement I recognized Bill Santry.

"Why, he's a friend of our'n, Bill--" Joan begun, but he interrupted her loudly and profanely: "Friend, hell! He's John Elkins' brother, and furthermore he's the one which is responsible for the crippled and mutilated condition in which you now sees me!"

Joan said nothing. She turned and looked at me in a very pecooliar manner, and then dropped her eyes shyly to the ground.

"Now, Joan," I begun, when all at once I saw what she was looking for. One of the men had dropped a Winchester before he run off. Her first bullet knocked off my hat as I forked Cap'n Kidd, and her second, third and fourth missed me so close I felt their hot wind. Then Cap'n Kidd rounded a curve with his belly to the ground, and my busted romance was left far behind me....

A couple of days later a mass of heartaches and bruises which might of been recognized as Breckinridge Elkins, the pride of Bear Creek, rode slowly down the trail that led to the settlements on the afore-said creek. And as I rode, it was my fortune to meet my brother John coming up the trail on foot.

"Where you been?" he greeted me hypocritically. "You look like you been rasslin' a pack of mountain lions."

I eased myself down from the saddle and said without heat: "John, just what was it that Bill Santry promised you?"

"Oh," says John with a laugh, "I skinned him in a hoss-trade before I left Cougar Paw, and he promised if he ever met me, he'd give me the lickin' of my life. I'm glad you don't hold no hard feelin's, Breck. It war just a joke, me sendin' you up there. You can take a joke, cain't you?"

"Sure," I said. "By the way, John, how's yore toe?"

"It's all right," says he.

"Lemme see," I insisted. "Set yore foot on that stump."

He done so and I give it a awful belt with the butt of my Winchester.

"That there is a receipt for yore joke," I grunted, as he danced around on one foot and wept and swore. And so saying, I mounted and rode on in gloomy grandeur. A Elkins always pays his debts.

www.ingramcontent.com/pod-product-compliance
Lightning Source LLC
Chambersburg PA
CBHW032213190626
46810CB00019B/3272